WHITE FANG

The Young Collector's
Illustrated Classics

WHITE FANG

By
Jack London

Adapted by
D.J. Arneson

Illustrated by
Karen Walker

Contents

CHAPTER

THE SHE-WOLF

The vast land was cold and lifeless. Two men struggled down a frozen river lined by a forest as dark as midnight. They churned through knee-deep snow, guiding a string of wolfish dogs. A birch-bark sled scraped over the snow behind the toiling dogs. It carried a coffin containing the mortal remains of a man who had failed to survive the Wild.

A faint cry cut through the sunless sky. "They're after us, Bill," the fur-covered man in front said.

"Meat is scarce," his companion said. He studied the fading light. "Better make camp."

They ate their beans in silence around a blazing fire. The night would be long. They stared into the blackness surrounding them.

"They're closer every night, Henry," Bill said. "The dogs are gettin' spooky." He gulped. "By the way, how many dogs we got?"

"Six," Henry answered.

Bill cocked his ear to the silent forest. "I saw seven."

Henry glanced at the dogs. They were huddled so close to the fire in fear it singed their hair. "There's only six," he said uneasily.

Bill wiped his mouth with the back of his hand. "I gave out seven fish," he said. "One dog ain't here. I saw it run into the woods."

They both looked into the velvet darkness. "You think it was—one of them?"

A mournful wail echoed through the night. Bill nodded. "I know it was," he said.

"How many cartridges do you have left in the rifle?" Henry asked quietly.

"Three," he whispered. "But three hundred would be better."

In the morning, Bill stirred the smoking embers. "Fatty's gone," he said flatly as Henry crawled from beneath his blankets.

Only five dogs remained. The others had been eaten by the wolves.

The men did not speak all day. They drove themselves and their dog team without stopping until the sun faded once again and the cold Arctic night settled over them.

"I wish they'd find a moose an' leave

us alone," Bill said. He glanced up from their fire in time to see a dark shadow slink across the snow into the woods. "That thing looks more like a dog than a wolf," he said. "It's mighty tame to be sneakin' in here stealin' fish."

"If that's all it aims to steal," Henry added.

Henry's words foretold disaster. By next daylight, Frog, the strongest dog of the bunch, was gone. With only four dogs left, the men were forced to stop early, or wear the dogs out completely. That night they watched the moving shadows circle their fire.

"It's a she-wolf," Henry whispered as the bravest shadow moved boldly at the light's flickering edge. "A wolf that knows to come in when we feed the dogs."

"That wolf is a dog," Bill said. "And I'm going to get it before it finishes us."

The next morning, Spanker was gone. The men hitched the remaining dogs to the sled and started pulling once again for Fort McGurry, still many days travel away.

Henry spied a furry form trotting into view on the trail behind them. "It's the she-wolf," he said, uttering a low whistle to Bill.

"Strange color for a wolf," Bill said. "I never seen a red wolf before. Looks almost cinnamon." He shook a fist at the creature and shouted, but it showed no fear. The men were meat and the she-dog and the pack were starving. Bill called the dog team to a halt. "I'm going to shoot it, Henry. What do you say?"

Henry nodded. "You only got three cartridges," he said lowly.

Bill pulled his rifle from under the sled-lashing. Instantly the she-wolf leaped into the forest and was gone. "She knows shootin' irons," he muttered. "But I'll get her, soon's I see the chance, or my name ain't Bill."

The dogs wearied early, and the men set up camp. The wolves circled nearer than ever, as bold as moths around a candle.

"Sailors talk of sharks followin' their

ships," Bill remarked as he crawled under his blankets after piling the fire high with fresh wood. "They're just waitin' their time, Henry. They're goin' to get us."

The next day, bad luck beset the men. The sled overturned on an icy rock. One-Ear, eager from the first day to join the she-wolf, broke free. He raced away. Within minutes a yelp shattered the silence. One-Ear, expecting companionship, instead became dinner.

"That does it," Bill shouted, reaching for his rifle. "They won't get any more of our dogs." He trudged into the under-brush. "It's a dead shot," he called. "I can't miss." He headed in a line that in a few minutes would put him in front of the cir-cling pack of voracious wolves.

"Don't take chances, Bill!" Henry warned.

Bill disappeared into the brush. Henry waited, listening to the silence. There was a shot. Then two more. The woods erupted with the snarls of wild beasts. Then, the silence returned.

Henry was alone now. Bill would not be coming back. Henry rose wearily. He righted the sled and hooked up the two remaining dogs. He put a line to his own shoulder and began to pull. The sled moved slowly. He did not look back.

He did not go far. By mid-afternoon the light began to fade. Henry spent the time before darkness piling high a lot of

dry firewood. He lit a roaring fire. He fed the dogs and ate his supper. He pulled his blanket over him. His two dogs whimpered at the closing circle of gaunt-ribbed wolves. Henry could not sleep. The danger was too close.

By morning Henry was desperate for sleep. He ate quickly. The wolves slipped back into the forest at daybreak, but they would never be far away. Henry cut a number of saplings and lashed them into a makeshift scaffold high between two tree trunks. "They got Bill," he said as he tugged the coffin to the scaffold. "And they might get me." He shouldered the pine box up onto the scaffold, safe from harm. "But they won't get the young fellow in here whose troubles are already over."

With the coffin safe, Henry hitched the two dogs to the lightened sled and set off for the safety of Fort McGurry. The wolves

quickly fell in behind him. Their red tongues flashed over sharp, glistening fangs. He stopped by mid-day to have enough time to chop an enormous stack of wood for the night's campfire.

He fought off the wolves by throwing flaming brands at them. By daylight he was exhausted. He tried to take the trail, but as soon as he left the safety of the fire, they leaped at him. He was trapped. He extended the fire to a giant dead tree that would provide more fuel. Nightfall came. The fire roared. The wolves repeated their bold attacks of the night before.

Henry slipped into sleep. He awakened with a start. The she-wolf stood over him. Her jaws were opened wide. Henry shoved a flaming brand into it. She yelped and ran away. A wolf slashed his leg. He leaped into the fire. He scooped up flaming coals in his leather mittens and hurled them in all directions. The snow sizzled with red-hot rain. The wolves retreated.

"You ain't got me yet," Henry shouted with a shake of a smoking mitten.

He formed the fire into a circle around him. The wolf-pack settled outside the ring of flames. The she-wolf pointed her muzzle at the stars and howled. The terrified man and dogs shivered at the sound.

The fire burned down by morning. Henry's strength was gone. "I guess you can come and get me," he muttered. "I'm goin' to sleep." His eyes drifted shut as the she-wolf stared hungrily into his face.

Shouts awakened Henry. The wolves were gone. Six men driving dogsleds pulled up to the smouldering fire. They tucked him under thick furs and carried him to safety.

As the men's shouts died away, another sound pierced the cold winter air. It was the wolf pack. They had found dinner and had moved in for the kill. Soon they would once again be roaming the Wild, following instincts as old as the North country itself.

CHAPTER 2

THE BATTLE OF THE FANGS

The pack's leader was a large gray wolf. He followed the she-wolf, who ran far ahead. The gray leader did not mind, but if he bumped into her, she snarled to warn him away. He accepted the scolding without anger. The other wolves trailed behind. The she-wolf slowed her pace so the pack could catch up.

Old One-Eye, a grizzled wolf who had seen many battles, ran on the she-wolf's right side. His right eye was gone. When he bumped the she-wolf, she snapped at him, too.

A young, spirited wolf followed the three. He tested their right to lead by edg-

ing between the gray leader and the she-wolf. Their sharp teeth quickly returned him to his place. He stayed close, waiting for the day he would lead.

The pack roamed together because food was scarce. The strongest ran in front. The weak, old, and very young followed. They ran without stopping. Without food, they would die. Forty hungry mouths snapped dryly in the cold, crisp air of the bitter Arctic winter.

At last, the forest yielded a moose. The wolves ate, and after they ate, they slept. Soon more food fell to the pack's sharp teeth. The famine ended. The pack split, two by two, male and female, until only the she-wolf, the gray leader, old One-Eye, and the ambitious young wolf remained.

The three males fought for the she-wolf's attention. The fighting grew worse day by day.

One day, the young wolf attacked old One-Eye's blind side. He clamped his teeth sharply over the old wolf's ear and shredded it to ribbons. The old wolf was wise in

the ways of warfare. He turned on the young wolf.

The gray leader saw his chance. He joined old One-Eye's attack against the young wolf. The she-wolf watched the older wolves destroy the upstart.

The gray leader turned away for an instant. Old One-Eye struck at the gray leader's exposed throat like a bolt of furred lightning. The thick vein in the gray leader's neck opened. His life gushed onto the snow, staining it bright red.

Old One-Eye walked proudly to the she-wolf's side. They sniffed noses. After that they ran side by side. Soon, the she-wolf began looking for a special place that only she would recognize.

One night as they ran beneath the glow of a bright moon, they came upon an Indian camp. Old One-Eye watched dumbly as man-animals moved among skin lodges. The camp was familiar to the she-wolf. She was comfortable near it, but old One-Eye was not. A gunshot drove them away.

CHAPTER

THE
GRAY CUB

The she-wolf found a deep, dry cave in a clay bank above the frozen Mackenzie River. It was a dark, round chamber with a flat, earthen floor. She entered and lay down. It would be her lair. One-Eye would sleep at the entrance.

Spring arrived. Running water and chirping birds were signs that the long winter was over. The she-wolf was content to remain in the cave while old One-Eye hunted food.

One day, strange sounds greeted old One-Eye's return. He stepped into the cave. Five tiny wolf cubs lay against the she-wolf's furry belly. She growled. Wolf

fathers sometimes ate their newborn. She watched old One-Eye closely. He turned away. It was his duty to hunt meat.

Miles from the lair, he found a fresh track. It led him to a female lynx patiently waiting for a porcupine to unroll. She struck the porcupine and caught a noseful of quills. She shrieked in pain as she ran into the forest. Old One-Eye killed the porcupine and carried it to the cave.

One cub was different from the others. Their fur was reddish, like the she-wolf's. His was gray, like his father's. He was identical to his father. He was physically a true wolf and the fiercest of the litter.

The gray cub was busy in his earthen home. He smelled its odors and studied its walls. One wall was bright with light. The others were dark. Old One-Eye could step through the wall of light. The cub was eager to try.

Famine returned to the Wild. Game was scarce. The she-wolf's milk stopped. One-Eye often returned with nothing to show for a day-long hunt. The cubs grew weak with hunger.

One day, the gray cub awoke to silence. His brothers and sisters were gone. The kills that old One-Eye brought back now went to him. He grew stronger. The famine was almost over.

Soon after, old One-Eye left the cave and never returned. The she-wolf found signs of his last battle near the lynx's lair. He had been no match for the fierce cat. Old One-Eye met his fate, and the lynx's kittens had a meal. The she-wolf avoided the lynx's lair after that. Both mothers had cubs to protect. She would not risk her life unless she had to.

CHAPTER

4

THE
LAW OF MEAT

Many days passed. The gray cub grew stronger and bolder. The wall of light tempted him. His mother's warnings grew dim. On a day that she was hunting for food, he carefully approached the wall.

The light hurt his eyes. He felt dizzy. He inched forward. In a burst of magic, the wall of light vanished. He was on the other side. A world of trees and mountains filled his vision. He took a bold step and tumbled down the slope. He landed in a heap. He ki-yi'd and yelped, but he wasn't hurt. The world was still there, and he was still in it.

The cub clambered over the rough

ground. His confidence grew. A bird
hopped near his nose. He stretched forward to sniff. The bird pecked him soundly.
It was a lesson that was followed by many
more. He learned the difference between

earth and water after falling into a stream. He learned to walk quietly when his noisy footsteps flushed a hidden rabbit. He learned to hunt by stalking a ptarmigan chick.

The chick was his first kill. It was a lesson that stood out from all the others. He was a hunter and killer. The Wild was not his enemy. The Wild was his domain.

The cub roamed longer and farther each day. He came to know his strengths and weaknesses and when to be bold or cautious. Encounters with other creatures were welded into his memory, adding to his wisdom of the Wild.

Soon the famine returned. The she-wolf hunted until she was rib thin. The cub ventured out of the cave, not to play, but to hunt. His prey were tiny mice.

One day the cub's mother returned with a baby lynx in her mouth. It was from the lair up the river's left fork. She and the young cub shared it.

Soon after, the kitten's mother appeared at the cave's entrance. She had tracked the she-wolf to avenge her kitten's death. The she-wolf leaped through the wall of light. The cub followed boldly.

The two adults fought viciously. Fur

flew. Blood spattered the ground. The gray cub clamped his small jaws over the lynx's rear leg and hung on for his life. The two huge creatures rolled over him, mashing

him to the ground. The cub's grip failed. The lynx was able to swat him with her paw. The little brave cub flew headlong into the wall. He yelped with pain, but he jumped up and ran back into the fight to help his mother. His courage was renewed, and this time he held on.

The she-wolf fought bravely, even-though she was worn down from starvation. She knew she had to win this fight to save her cub. She swung around and grabbed the lynx by the throat. She tore the flesh with her teeth. The lynx stopped fighting and fell dead. The long battle was over at last.

The she-wolf licked her cub's wounds. Both wolves were weak. They ate their kill and rested.

The cub had fought a ferocious enemy and survived. He had eaten its flesh and it gave him life. It was his greatest lesson.

There were two kinds of life. He and his mother were one kind. Everything else was the other kind. It was the law of survival. It said: EAT OR BE EATEN!

White Fang

The gray cub was happy to be alive. He was a killer with one purpose—to survive. He would learn better how to survive in the months ahead.

For now, he rested and enjoyed not being hungry for once. The she-wolf, too, was relieved to get rest. She snuggled up to her little cub, and they both slept. They knew that soon they would have to hunt again.

CHAPTER

5

THE
BONDAGE

The cub left the cave to get a drink from the stream. He was sleepy and not paying attention. He stopped suddenly. An unfamiliar scent reached his sensitive nose. He blinked.

Sitting quietly on their haunches near the stream were five man-animals. They did not see him. He wanted to run away, but something deep inside changed his mind. He knew that men were the masters of the Wild.

The gray cub felt an urge to sit at the Indians' fire. It had been passed on to him through his mother's blood. It was a very strong urge.

An Indian walked to where the cub hugged the ground and extended a hand toward him. The hand was terrifying. The cub's hair bristled. He did not know if he should run or fight.

"Wabam wabisca ip pit tah," the Indian said. "Look at the white fangs." He reached for the cub. The cub struck. He sank his fangs into the hand. Another hand knocked the cub loose. The cub whimpered loudly.

Crashing underbrush parted and the she-wolf leaped into the clearing to save

her cub. She jumped between the cub and the circle of startled men. Her menacing snarl warned of the bite that would follow.

"Kiche!" an Indian shouted.

The she-wolf wilted.

"Kiche!" the man repeated.

The she-wolf curled her tail between her legs. She crouched until her belly scraped the ground. Her snarl melted. She wagged her tail wildly as a sign of peace. She let the Indians rub her head and scratch her back.

The cub watched in awe. He was right. Man-animals were masters of the Wild. The same hands that hit could also inspire feelings he did not yet understand. He crouched next to his mother.

"It is Kiche," Gray Beaver said. "Her mother was a dog, but her father was a wolf." The she-wolf had belonged to him. When the famine struck, there was no meat for the dogs. The she-wolf ran away to survive on her own.

"She has lived with the wolves," Gray Beaver said. "This is the sign of it."

He put his hand on the cub.

"Kiche is his mother, but his father was a wolf. In him is little dog but much wolf. And he is mine."

Gray Beaver held up the cub. The

cub's lips parted. His little fangs glistened.

"His fangs be white," Gray Beaver said. "White Fang shall be his name."

Gray Beaver tied Kiche, the she-wolf, to a tree with a string of rawhide. White Fang lay down beside her. He let the Indians pet him, but the sight of their hands still frightened him.

The clearing filled as the tribe of forty men, women, and children arrived. They were laden with gear. Dogs, with bags tied to their backs, trailed them. White Fang had never seen dogs before.

The dogs rushed forward when they saw the wolves. Kiche leaped between them and her cub. The Indians beat the dogs back with clubs.

White Fang licked his wounds. He was puzzled. The camp was filled with many of his own kind, and they were not at all friendly.

The Indians gathered their packs and dogs and set off. A tiny man-animal held Kiche's tether. White Fang followed behind his mother.

The tribe followed the stream through the valley. White Fang had never ranged so far. When they stopped at last, the Indians raised tepees and made their camp.

The Indian camp was a strange place to White Fang. Tepees were fearsome giants. Man-animals made odd noises. But the worst was one of his own kind, a puppy like himself, but older and bigger. He was a bully named Lip-lip.

The first time White Fang saw him, he tipped his head in friendly greeting. Lip-lip answered with an angry snarl. Lip-lip and White Fang circled one another. White Fang thought it was a game. Suddenly Lip-lip leaped in with teeth bared and slashed the gray cub's shoulder.

White Fang yelped, but anger drove him to fight. He rushed Lip-lip with his fangs bared.

Lip-lip had fought many puppy fights, and White Fang none. Lip-lip's bites chased White Fang to his mother's side. The fight ended. They would be enemies from now on.

Soon, the cub forgot his fear. His curiosity drew him on. He sniffed the air.

Gray Beaver was twirling a stick between the palms of his hands. A wisp of smoke rose from the stick. Gray Beaver sprinkled dry grass on the smoke. He blew. A flame leaped up the stick.

White Fang crawled toward the fire. He put his nose to it. It burned with the worst pain of his life. He leaped into the air with a yelp.

The Indians roared with laughter. White Fang knew it was aimed at him. He raced to his mother's side. She was the only creature in the camp who did not laugh.

That night, White Fang snuggled against his mother. He was homesick for his old life. He wanted to return to the cave. The man-animals had a power over him. They could make fire. They were gods.

White Fang learned the ways of the man-animals in the days that followed. Like Kiche, he rolled over when they ordered it and came when they called. He cowered with fear when they threatened him with a raised hand. In the end, White Fang belonged to the man-animals.

The cub also learned the ways of his kind. The puppies and dogs made his life miserable. The worst was Lip-lip, who picked on White Fang as his special enemy. White Fang fought back, but Lip-lip was too big and too much a bully. But White Fang's spirit grew, and so did his temper. His savage wolf blood became more savage under Lip-lip's tormenting.

White Fang's spirit was not broken when Lip-lip beat him. It became stronger, and he became mean. He was forced to grow up quickly to survive in a world that was against him. He learned his lessons well.

White Fang was very clever. He was still too small to beat Lip-lip, but there were other ways to find revenge. One day as Lip-lip strutted through camp, White Fang ran across his path as if he hadn't seen him. Lip-lip raced after White Fang, eager to show him who was king.

White Fang ran for his life as if he did not know where he was headed. He was a better runner than Lip-lip, but he held back so Lip-lip could keep up. Lip-lip followed blindly.

White Fang raced around a nearby tepee with Lip-lip hot on his heels, straight to where Kiche was tied. It was too late to

stop. The she-wolf knocked Lip-lip to the ground. She closed her strong jaws over his leg and shook him like a flopping fish until he dropped. Lip-lip wailed. His quivering legs would not move.

White Fang sank his fangs into the bully's leg. Lip-lip ran in shame to his own tepee. White Fang didn't stop snapping until squaws forced him back with a shower of stones. He trotted back to Kiche with his head held high.

The day came when Gray Beaver knew Kiche would not run away. He untied her. White Fang was overjoyed to run at her side as she roamed through the Indian camp. Lip-lip was always a danger, but as long as White Fang was with Kiche, he was safe.

Mother and puppy strayed to the edge of the thick woods bordering the campsite. White Fang led the way. He remembered their lair, the bubbling stream, and the quiet forest. He wanted to return. He ran ahead, but Kiche stood firm.

White Fang took a few more steps into the woods, but Kiche did not follow. Something was calling the puppy. But Kiche also heard a call. For her, the call to run at the side of the man-animals was stronger than the call White Fang heard. She turned from the forest and trotted back to the Indian camp.

White Fang sniffed the pine-scented breeze drifting from the forest depths. He still needed his mother. It was too early for him to be free.

However, White Fang's days with his mother were already numbered. Three Eagles was preparing for a long trip away from camp. He needed a dog. Gray Beaver owed a debt to Three Eagles. To settle it, he gave Three Eagles a strip of red cloth, some rifle cartridges, and Kiche.

White Fang watched from the river bank as Three Eagles paddled away in his

canoe. Kiche sat obediently in the frail craft. The puppy leaped into the water and swam after the canoe. Three Eagles batted him away with the paddle.

Gray Beaver paddled after White Fang in his own canoe. He grabbed him by the nape of his neck and tossed him in. He beat him soundly all the way back to shore. White Fang whimpered as the god who owned him gave him a lesson he would not forget.

A spark of freedom flickered and White Fang bit Gray Beaver's foot. The blows fell harder than ever.

On shore, White Fang followed his master obediently. Lip-lip was watching. It was his opportunity to get back at White Fang.

Lip-lip jumped at the puppy, who rolled to the ground, unable to defend himself. Lip-lip was ready to tear White Fang's flesh. Then, the same foot White Fang had bitten moments earlier shot forward to kick Lip-lip across the river bank. Lip-lip's attack was over.

White Fang trotted behind Gray Beaver. He understood that punishment was a right that belonged only to his master. Others were not permitted.

That night White Fang whimpered quietly for his mother. If he ran away to their lair, he would never see her again, but if he stayed with his master, she would come back. His bondage was complete.

CHAPTER

6

THE
OUTCAST

Lip-lip's torment did not stop. In defense, White Fang became more savage. His reputation grew. The man-animals saw him as a trouble-maker. Whenever there was mischief among the dogs, White Fang was always there. The Indians threw stones and said he would never be any good. So White Fang had no allies. He had to defend himself however he could.

He was no match for the pack of young dogs who followed Lip-lip. When they attacked him, he had to fight for his life. He had to develop special skills to survive, or he would die.

When the pack was on him, White

Fang had to keep on his feet at all costs. If he went down, the raging animals would show no mercy, but if he stayed standing, he could fight them off. His ability to stay upright exceeded that of a cat.

The growing wolf puppy also learned that he could not waste time bristling and snarling. When the other dogs prepared for a fight, they strutted and snapped to build courage. White Fang learned to attack at once to catch the others off their guard. He could slash an ear or tear a shoulder before his enemies were ready to fight back. Delay would mean defeat.

White Fang's quickness gave him another advantage. If he struck without warning, he could knock a dog off its feet. Once a dog lay defenseless, he could go for its throat.

One day White Fang spied a lone enemy at the edge of the woods. He launched his throat-attack, pitching the dog to the ground. He tore open the dog's neck and the dog died.

An Indian witnessed the attack. He

told the dead dog's master that White Fang killed his dog. Other Indians added their stories of White Fang's ferociousness.

Even though White Fang was stealing their meat and fighting their dogs only to

survive, the Indians saw him as a trouble-maker. He was hurting *their* ability to survive.

The Indians went to Gray Beaver's tepee to complain. White Fang watched the angry crowd through the open flap. Gray Beaver faced the tribe. He would not permit them to punish his dog. He was White Fang's only protector.

White Fang was an outcast. His own

kind rejected him and the Indians rebuked him. He was forced to be constantly on guard against an attack by fang or hand.

White Fang's snarl was fierce. He

bared his fangs. He wrinkled his snout. He opened his eyes so they glared like coals fanned on a fire. His hair bristled so he looked larger than life. His tongue flashed back and forth like the searching head of a deadly red snake. His ears flattened back, and saliva dripped from his curled lips. And from his throat he loosed a terrifying growl that stopped men and beasts in their tracks.

The dogs feared White Fang. They had to stay together for self protection. If one strayed from the pack, it was instantly in peril of death. Together the Indians and the dogs had created a terrible enemy, and the dogs often had to pay the price.

The fear he gave held no pleasure for White Fang because it was driven by hatred. The dogs and mankind were against him. He was the outsider. He was the outcast.

The fights and rebukes were proof of the code he had to live by: to obey the strong and oppress the weak. White Fang obeyed his master because Gray Beaver was strong. He destroyed members of the dog pack who were weak.

To survive, White Fang had to be stronger, swifter, craftier, deadlier, leaner, and tougher than all the rest. His muscles were like iron. His intelligence was razor-sharp. He had to be these things or he would die.

The Indians dismantled their camp for the fall hunt that would carry them through lean times. White Fang watched eagerly.

He was not going to leave. He would

slip into the woods. Freedom would be his at last.

As the canoes bobbed downstream, White Fang slinked away. He entered a stream that was beginning to freeze and ran until his trail was lost in a dense thicket. He fell asleep.

Gray Beaver's voice awakened him. Gray Beaver's squaw was also calling, and so was Mit-sah, Gray Beaver's young son. White Fang trembled. He thought he should go to them, but he stayed. The voices died away. When the day turned to dark, he emerged. He was free.

Something troubled him. He was lonely. The silent forest was frightening. Dark shadows loomed everywhere. The air was cold. Gray Beaver's warm tepee was gone. Memories of the camp and a blazing fire flickered in his mind. Thoughts of meat and fish made him hungry. He had made a terrible mistake.

His bondage had turned him soft. He was dependent on his master. Alone in the forest, he was uncertain of what to do. His

keen senses had lost their edge. White Fang felt that something awful was going to happen. He whimpered. He burst into a run. His feet flew over the earth.

Brush and branches tore at his fur. He ran headlong through the darkness. He wanted to smell campfire smoke. He wanted to hear familiar sounds. He burst into the clearing. The village was gone.

Shivering with fear, White Fang walked to the ring of packed earth where Gray Beaver's tepee had stood. He sat down. The clearing was abandoned. The site was as silent as the forest.

White Fang pointed his snout at the rising moon. His throat quivered. His mouth opened. His sorrows rushed over him like shadows.

He felt grief over losing his beloved Kiche...the misery of rejection by his own kind...the fear of danger that lay ahead. It all rose in his throat like a violent wind and burst into the night sky. A long, mournful wolf howl carried his terrors skyward. It was the first he had ever uttered.

The sun rose, but the loneliness of the abandoned camp was worse. White Fang leaped to his feet and ran to the river's edge. He turned sharply along the bank without stopping. He followed the channel carved by the river through the forest, past steep bluffs and over wider valleys.

White Fang ran through the day and

into the following night. His feet pads were cut and bleeding. His fur was torn in clumps from his hide. He was weak and hungry.

When snow began to fall and he could barely see what lay ahead, he had to struggle to keep on going. He began to limp, but he overcame the pain and did not stop.

Snow flew in thick clouds. White Fang held his nose to the ground, sniffing for a familiar scent. He spied fresh footprints.

He ran alongside the track, never letting it out of his sight. Familiar sounds struck his ears. A flickering light burst through the darkness.

There was Kloo-kooch, roasting meat over a friendly fire as Gray Beaver munched raw tallow.

White Fang shrank toward the ground. He laid his ears back and tucked his tail between his legs. He slinked into camp, expecting a beating.

Gray Beaver saw him. The Indian said nothing. White Fang inched along the ground to his master's feet. He lay his head down and waited for his punishment.

The blow did not come. White Fang lifted his eyes. Gray Beaver's hand was over his head, but it was not clenched. It held a piece of tallow. White Fang ate this offering, and Gray Beaver called for fresh meat.

Soon White Fang was full. He lay at Gray Beaver's feet, basking in the glow of the fire. His eyes closed, and he drifted off to sleep. He felt content and no longer lonely.

When the sun rose the next day, he would be with his master. He had given himself over to the man-animals, the gods. He was theirs.

CHAPTER

7

THE FAMINE

In December, Gray Beaver and his family journeyed up the Mackenzie River. He drove one sled and Mit-sah, his son, drove another. Mit-sah's sled was a small, birch-bark toboggan with no runners. White Fang and the other puppies were harnessed to the sled.

Lip-lip was now Mit-sah's dog. Mit-sah disliked Lip-lip for bullying White Fang. He made Lip-lip's life miserable by making Lip-lip the team leader. It was not a position of honor because, to the other dogs, the front dog looked as if he were running away. Also, Mit-sah fed Lip-lip first, so the other dogs hated him even more.

The dogs stayed out of White Fang's way. But if a dog challenged him, he quickly settled the matter with a furious but short fight. White Fang was an animal to be avoided.

As the months passed, White Fang grew stronger and wiser. His world was a cold, brutal place with no place for kindness. He had been hurt too much for that. Gray Beaver was his master, but the dog had no affection for his god. White Fang did not know that a man's hand could hold kindness as easily as it could hold a club, so he was suspicious of them. There were some things about man-animals White Fang still did not know.

The Indians were camped at Great Slave Lake. As White Fang foraged among the tepees for food, he saw a boy chopping frozen moose meat with an axe. He snapped up a fallen meat chip.

The boy raised a club to hit him. White Fang ran. The boy trapped him between two tepees. The boy raised his club.

White Fang jumped at the hand. His fangs tore open the flesh. This was a law he knew he should not break. Animals were not allowed to bite the gods. White Fang ran to Gray Beaver and cowered between his master's legs.

Gray Beaver did not let the Indians punish White Fang for biting the boy. White Fang understood there was a difference between the gods. Gray Beaver was his god. The others were not. He had to accept what his gods gave him, but he did not have to accept anything from the other gods, especially injustice.

That same day, Mit-sah was gathering wood. The boy White Fang had bitten found him. He and his friends attacked Mit-sah as White Fang watched. It was not his business to interfere in a god's matters. Then he realized Mit-sah was one of his gods. He leaped on the band of boys and drove them off screaming.

When Mit-sah and White Fang returned home, Gray Beaver gave White Fang an extra large helping of meat as a

reward. The incident taught White Fang to protect his gods and their property. In exchange, White Fang received food, warmth, protection, and companionship. It was a simple bargain, but it cost him his liberty. His allegiance to man was complete.

In April, Gray Beaver's journey back to his home village was over. White Fang was one year old. He was trim and muscular. His coat was the true gray of a wolf, and he looked like a wolf. He was only one-quarter dog. He did not look like his mother, but his mind was like hers.

Except for Lip-lip, White Fang was the largest dog, big enough and wise enough to deal with dogs like Baseek, a grizzled old-timer. In days past, Baseek could drive White Fang away by baring his fangs. But the old dog had grown weaker while White Fang grew stronger.

One day the two met face to face over the bones of a freshly killed moose. White Fang grabbed a shinbone and dragged it

into a thicket to gnaw on. Baseek watched with envy. He rushed into the thicket after the prize.

White Fang did not hesitate. He leaped at Baseek and slashed him twice. Baseek was dumbfounded. He backed away. White Fang stood over the raw bone with his hair bristling. Baseek raised the hair on his back and stared ferociously at the bold yearling.

For a moment White Fang paused. When he was a puppy, Baseek's anger was not taken lightly. He was ready to back off and not fight, but Baseek stepped toward the bone.

It was a careless move. White Fang had not given up the bone yet. The younger dog stood his ground.

Baseek presumed the prize was his. He grabbed the bone, and White Fang struck. He knocked the old dog to the ground. He tore Baseek's ears to ribbons. He slashed his throat. The old fighter struggled to his feet, stunned by the bold attack. Youth had overtaken age.

The victory changed White Fang's image of himself. He walked more boldly. By summer, all the dogs stayed out of White Fang's way.

A new tepee stood at the edge of the Indian camp when White Fang returned from a moose hunt with Gray Beaver. He stopped abruptly at the sight of a full-grown dog in the teepee's entrance. It was Kiche, his mother. He remembered her, but Kiche did not remember her son at all. She snarled.

The sound revived White Fang's memories. Pleasant feelings of his cubhood returned. He once had been the center of Kiche's attention, and he still longed for that faraway time. He rushed toward his mother joyously.

Kiche slashed him. The startled young dog fell back. His cheek was torn and bloody. He did not know a wolf-mother does not remember her cubs after they are grown.

A new litter milled around Kiche's feet. White Fang backed away. His memories of the lair faded. White Fang had no place in Kiche's life anymore. He turned and walked away.

White Fang grew wise and powerful on his own. If he had stayed in the Wild, his wolf nature would have become stronger. But he lived with the man-animals and became more dog-like. He was strong in all things, except one. He could not stand being laughed at. Men's laughter turned him into a raging demon.

When he was three years old, White Fang felt famine once again. The Mackenzie Indians faced starvation. Fish vanished from the river, caribou were scarce, the moose were gone, and even rabbits were rare. Old or weak Indians and many children died. Hunters returned with nothing to show for their hunt. They turned to the dogs and ate them. Some dogs ran away, but they did not last long in the Wild. Dogs were no match for wolves.

White Fang had skills the others did not. He knew how to hunt to survive. He

ran off and stalked his prey for hours. He waited patiently by a track for a squirrel or rabbit to appear. He did not let his hunger rule him. He waited until a kill was certain. Then he leaped.

White Fang's wanderings took him back to the valley of his birth. The old cave was still there, cut deep into the bank he had tumbled down on his first venture into the world. A wolf was inside. It was Kiche.

She, too, had run away to escape the famine. At her side was a wobbly, starving cub. Its days were nearly over. The weak did not survive the perils of starvation.

Mother and son faced one another for the last time. Kiche snarled menacingly. White Fang did not mind. He was now old enough that he no longer needed her. He turned away and continued his trek.

By summer, the famine ended. White Fang was strong and in splendid condition. As he trotted along a streambed, he came face-to-face with Lip-lip. The older dog had not fared well.

The hair on the dogs' backs rose. Their lips parted. Lip-lip was not eager to fight. White Fang's tactic was to attack without warning.

White Fang's bared teeth sank into Lip-lip's throat. His jaws closed tight. Lip-lip struggled, but it was no use. His life slowly ebbed away.

White Fang strutted around Lip-lip's

body once and then continued on his way.

A few days later, White Fang reached the river. An Indian village stood on land that had been bare. Familiar sights met his eyes. Remembered smells reached his nose. Sounds he knew touched his ears.

The famine was over. Fish were cooking. The man-animals and children were laughing. The village was a happy place once more.

White Fang trotted straight to Gray Beaver's tepee. Kloo-kooch welcomed him with food and glad cries.

Content to be home, White Fang lay down to wait for Gray Beaver to return.

CHAPTER

8

THE
MAD GOD

White Fang was made leader of the dog-sled team, separating him from his own kind forever. The other dogs hated him, and he them. He had to run, because if he stopped to fight, Mit-sah's whip would turn him back. So he ran at the head of the pack, anger filling him every step of the way.

The dogs learned to leave White Fang alone when they were pulling the sled because they feared his wrath as much as the stinging whip.

It was different in camp. Mit-sah's whip was not there to enforce order. The dogs were free to pursue White Fang. But only in a pack. He could kill them all, one-by-one, but it would be his life if they attacked him all at once. He was fast and wise enough to protect himself, and he did, many times over. Each time, his hatred of dogs increased. It was his will to destroy them all, wherever he found them.

When White Fang was almost five years old, Gray Beaver took him to the Yukon. White Fang fought every strange dog that challenged him. The dogs didn't know about his hatred. They didn't know about his lightning-quick throat attack. White Fang's growing reputation as a fierce fighter spread far and wide.

Gray Beaver and White Fang arrived at Fort Yukon in the summer of 1898. The Hudson's Bay Company's fort was there. So were many Indians and more excitement than could be found in all the Northland.

Thousands of gold-hunters stopped at Fort Yukon on the way to Dawson and the Klondike, hundreds of miles farther north. The gold rush was on. Gray Beaver's sled was loaded with furs, mittens, and moccasins. Careful trading with the prospectors made Gray Beaver rich.

White Fang saw his first white men. They were different from the Indians. He sensed their power. If the Indians were gods, so were the white men. He watched these new gods from a safe distance. When he saw that they treated their own dogs well, he ventured closer.

White Fang was different from their dogs. His wolfish appearance made him stand out. One look at the wolf-dog's bared fangs was warning enough to leave him alone.

Few white men lived at Fort Yukon. They arrived by steamer and spent only a short time before continuing their journey. White Fang soon learned that their dogs did not know how to fight. They attacked him the minute they stepped off the steamboat. He knocked them to the ground and finished them with a throat-attack if they weren't saved by an irate master.

The white men living at Fort Yukon enjoyed watching White Fang destroy the

unsuspecting dogs from the Southland. They hooted and hollered, as dog after dog met his end or was hastened back aboard the steamboat.

Beauty Smith enjoyed the brutal sport more than the others. He was the ugliest

man in the North and a weak, sniveling coward. His job was to cook and clean for the others. He wanted White Fang for himself.

White Fang sensed the evil in Beauty Smith. He knew his crooked smile and soft voice only covered the man's dark soul.

Beauty Smith wanted to buy White Fang, but Gray Beaver refused to sell. He was already rich from trading. There was no other dog like White Fang in all the North. He was the best sled-dog and the fiercest fighter. Beauty Smith licked his lips.

Beauty Smith was crafty. He returned to Gray Beaver's camp with bottles of whiskey. Soon Gray Beaver needed more. After a time, Gray Beaver no longer controlled his own will and would do anything to get more liquor.

After Gray Beaver's money was gone, Beauty Smith offered to buy White Fang for bottles of whiskey. Gray Beaver's dimmed eyes glistened.

"You ketch um dog you take um all

right," he said. Beauty Smith handed over the bottles, and White Fang belonged to a madman.

White Fang ran back to Gray Beaver's camp the first night. Beauty Smith dragged him back the next day and beat him fiercely with a heavy club. He beat White Fang senseless.

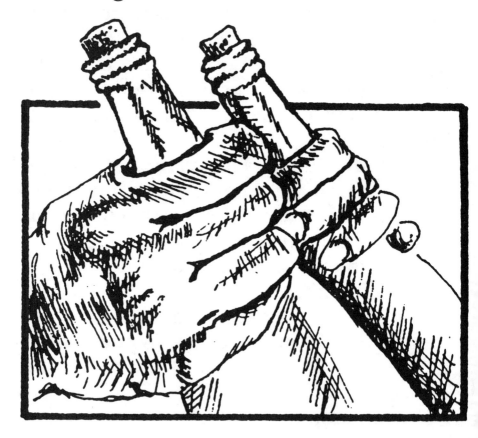

White Fang

Beauty Smith enjoyed torturing White Fang. The lowest of the low and despised by men, he took out his anger on White Fang.

Each time White Fang escaped, Beauty Smith got him back. The beatings took their toll. A weaker dog would have died. White Fang did not die, but in the end he was forced to go with his new master. When Gray Beaver left the fort, penniless and broken, the dog stayed behind, a captive of a white god more terrible than any creature found in the Wild.

CHAPTER

9

THE
CLINGING DEATH

Beauty Smith chained White Fang in a pen. He brutalized the dog by teasing and beating him. Soon White Fang was a fiend. He was no longer just an enemy of his own kind. Now he was an enemy to everyone. His hate grew. But most of all, he hated Beauty Smith.

The reason for Beauty Smith's treatment of White Fang was revealed one day when a group of men gathered around his pen. White Fang snarled at them. The men laughed. They would not have laughed if the pen didn't protect them. White Fang was over five feet long and two and a half feet high at the shoulder. He was solid muscle and weighed over ninety pounds, far more than a wolf of the same size. He was a fierce fighting animal, and he was in perfect condition.

The pen door flew open, and a huge dog was shoved inside. White Fang leaped at him, tearing a deep wound in the animal's neck.

The dog shook its head in surprise. It plunged forward, but White Fang was already out of the way. He slashed the invading dog's flesh again. It was no match.

White Fang would have killed the dog if Beauty Smith hadn't stepped in with a club and beat him away. The men exchanged money. Beauty Smith ended up with a fistful.

Large sums of money were bet on White Fang's fights as his reputation spread across the land. Beauty Smith hung a sign on his cage. People paid fifty cents just to see "The Fighting Wolf."

White Fang never knew defeat. His lightning quickness and sure footing made

THE
FIGHTING
DOG

him the winner every time. Soon there
were no dogs left to match White Fang's
fighting skills.

Beauty Smith was unable to arrange
dog fights for his wolf-dog. Rather than
stop the blood from flowing, Beauty Smith
pitted wolves against White Fang.

Once, Beauty Smith put a full-grown

female lynx in the cage. White Fang barely survived the battle. The lynx was White Fang's last fight for awhile, though, because there were no other opponents.

Beauty Smith kept White Fang caged until the next spring when a stranger with a dog unlike any ever seen in the Klondike arrived. A fight was arranged. Nobody talked about anything else.

On the day of the fight, Beauty Smith shoved White Fang into the center of a clearing surrounded by curious, shouting men. The other dog was already there. It was a bulldog.

For the first time in his life, White Fang did not attack. He stared at the odd-looking beast. He had never seen a dog like it.

The bulldog's owner, Tim Keenan, shouted "Go to it." The squat animal waddled into the center of the ring and blinked at White Fang. The crowd roared for the fight to begin. "Sic 'em, Cherokee," a man shouted. "Go get 'im, Cherokee," another called.

The bulldog wagged his stumpy tail. He wasn't afraid, but he was quite lazy. Besides that, White Fang did not look right to the bulldog. Cherokee was waiting for the fighting dog to show up.

Tim Keenan kneeled over Cherokee. He rubbed the dog's fur the wrong way. Cherokee began to growl.

White Fang watched and listened. The hair on his back raised. He was ready.

Tim Keenan shoved Cherokee. The bulldog ambled jerkily forward on his short bow-legs, and White Fang struck. The crowd screamed. The fight was on.

White Fang slashed the bulldog's neck, but Cherokee didn't seem to notice. The wolf-dog attacked again. He tore off a piece of the bulldog's ear. White Fang could only slash when he attacked, because the bulldog was too low to the ground for him to get a grip on its throat.

White Fang was puzzled. He had never fought a dog that did not fight back. The bulldog seemed unable to defend itself. Cherokee was bleeding. His neck was torn. His ears were tatters. He plodded after White Fang. He moved quickly when he wanted to, but White Fang always leaped out of the way. Cherokee was waiting for the right time.

White Fang tried one more time to knock the short, heavyset dog down. It was a mistake. White Fang raced toward Cherokee. His speed was too great. He was too tall for the squat bulldog. He struck Cherokee but flew right over the dog's back. He somersaulted through the air and

landed on his side. It was the first time in his fighting history that he ever lost his footing.

Cherokee made his move. Before White Fang could regain his feet, the bulldog was on him. His powerful jaws closed over White Fang's throat in a grip that could not be broken.

White Fang shook wildly. The bulldog clung to his neck like an giant leech. White Fang dragged the heavy dog around the clearing. The bulldog's weight slowed him down, sapping his strength. White Fang was confused. Dogs did not fight like this.

Cherokee clung tightly as White Fang spun in circles. His grip was not close enough to the throat to kill, so each time the wolf-dog paused for breath, Cherokee inched his jaws forward. He would hang there until White Fang went insane, or died.

The dogs fell to the ground. White Fang landed on his back. Cherokee was on top. White Fang clawed at Cherokee's soft underbelly with his hind legs. Cherokee

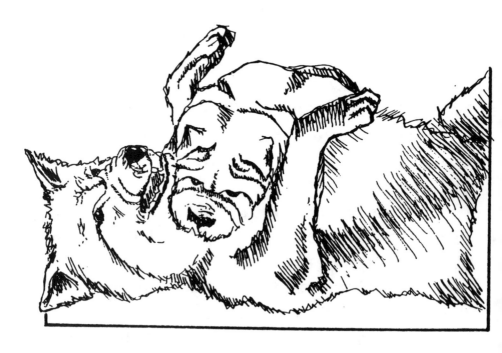

rolled off. His grip on White Fang's neck inched closer to the jugular vein throbbing in the wolf-dog's throat. White Fang was tiring. The battle was nearly over. Death would be sudden.

The screaming crowd placed last minute bets. Beauty Smith saw his dog was beaten. He leaped into the ring, pointing a scornful finger at the struggling dog. He laughed fiendishly into White Fang's face.

White Fang's rage erupted. He ran around and around the ring with the fifty pound bulldog clinging to his throat. "Cherokee! Cherokee!" the crowd roared. This enraged White Fang even more.

But anger and hate were no match against the clinging death. White Fang's strength was nearly gone. He trembled. He ceased struggling.

A shout went up. Two sleds driven by dog-mushers from the Northern gold fields rumbled full-speed down the trail. They stopped near the circle of men. A handsome young man saw the death struggle. He leaped from his sled and ran into the crowd.

Beauty Smith was not interested in the new arrivals. He had seen White Fang's eyes start to glaze. He knew the fight was over. He jumped into the ring and kicked furiously at White Fang who was unable to move. The crowd roared disapproval, but that didn't stop Beauty Smith.

The young man pushed his way into the ring. His fist shot square into Beauty

Smith's jaw. Beauty Smith dropped to the ground.

"You cowards!" the young man shouted. "You beasts!"

The man was outraged. His eyes

flashed with anger at all who stood around White Fang and the bulldog.

Beauty Smith struggled to his feet. The man knocked him down again. This time the coward did not get up.

"Lend a hand, Matt," the young man said.

The newcomers bent over the dogs. While Matt held White Fang, the young man grabbed Cherokee's jaws to pry them

open. They would not budge. "Beasts!" he shouted at the crowd.

"It's no use, Mr. Scott," Matt said. "You can't break 'em apart that way."

"Won't some of you help?" Scott called to the men. Nobody answered. Scott drew his pistol. He stuck the cold barrel into Cherokee's mouth and twisted. The steel grated against the dog's teeth.

"Don't break them teeth," Tim Keenan warned.

"I'll break his neck if I have to," Scott answered. He twisted the barrel sharply. The jaws parted. Matt carefully worked White Fang's flesh out of the locked jaws. The dogs were parted at last.

"Take him away," Scott demanded. Tim Keenan dragged his bulldog into the crowd.

White Fang wobbled to his feet but instantly fell back to the ground.

"Just about finished," Matt said.

Beauty Smith stood over the men and the wolf-dog. Scott stared at him with fire in his eyes. "How much is a good sled dog worth, Matt?"

"Three hundred dollars."

"One that's all chewed up?"

"Half of that," Matt said.

Scott opened his purse and counted out one hundred and fifty dollars in gold. He flung it at Beauty Smith. "I'm buying your dog, you beast," he hissed.

"I ain't a-sellin'," Beauty Smith said.

Scott clenched his fist. "Yes, you are," he said. "Here's your money. The dog is mine."

Beauty Smith scurried away.

Scott and Matt loaded White Fang onto a sled and drove off.

"Who was that?" Cherokee's owner asked a man in the dwindling crowd.

"That's Weedon Scott, one of them crack-a-jack mining experts. He's not someone to mess with, mister. He's some-body special."

CHAPTER

10

THE LOVING MASTER

"It's hopeless," Weedon Scott said to Matt, as they sat on the step of Scott's cabin. White Fang snarled at the sled dogs from the end of a taut chain. "There's no taming a wolf."

"I'm not so sure," Matt said.

"What do you mean by that?" Scott asked.

"Wolf or dog, he's been tamed before," the dog-musher said, pointing at White Fang's chest. "See them harness marks?"

"You're right, Matt. He was a sled dog before Beauty Smith got him."

"Could be he's still a sled dog," Matt said.

The hope in Scott's eyes faded quickly. He shook his head. "No. We've had him two weeks, and he's wilder than ever."

Matt rubbed his jaw. "Give 'im a chance. Turn him loose for a spell. But carry a club."

Scott was doubtful. "You try it."

The dog-musher found a heavy club. He approached White Fang carefully. White Fang's eyes were on the club.

"You see him watch the club," Matt said. "That's a good sign. Means he won't go for me as long as I got it handy."

Matt grasped White Fang's collar. The dog snarled, but he did not attack. Matt removed the collar.

White Fang could not believe he was free. He walked away slowly, unsure if the club would strike at any moment. Nothing happened. He returned to his original spot.

"Won't he run away?" Scott asked.

"Got to take that chance," Matt said.

"Poor devil," Scott said. "He needs human kindness."

Scott entered the cabin and returned

with a piece of meat. He tossed it to White Fang.

Major, one of the sled dogs, spied the meat. He jumped for it. White Fang attacked at once. His teeth tore the surprised dog's throat.

Scott shook his head. "It's a pity," he said, "But I have to say he deserved it."

Matt lashed out at White Fang with a swift kick. White Fang jumped aside. His teeth closed on the man's leg.

"He got me," Matt grumbled.

"I told you it was hopeless," Scott said. He was discouraged. It had not worked out

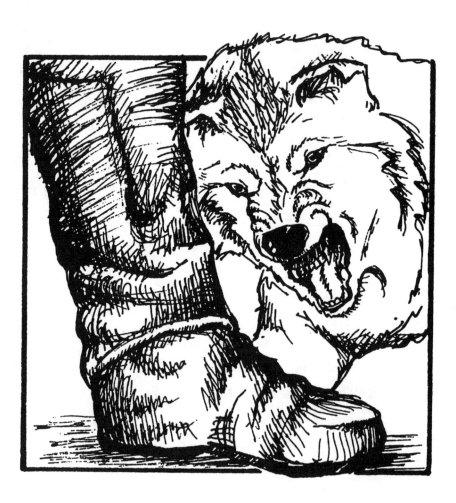

the way he hoped. "We gave it a try. There's nothing left to do now."

He drew his revolver, but Matt stopped him.

"He's been through hell, Mr. Scott. He can't change into an angel in a minute. Give 'im time."

Major lay dying on the snow. Matt's own leg was bleeding. Scott shook his head. "But look what he's already done."

"Served Major right," the dog-musher said. "He tried to steal White Fang's meat. A dog that won't fight to protect its own meat ain't worth saving. White Fang did the right thing."

"We've got to draw the line," Scott argued. "It would be a mercy to kill him."

"Give the poor devil a chance, Mr. Scott," Matt said. "This is the first time he's been free. If he don't come around, I'll kill him myself."

Scott looked at White Fang and put away the pistol. He made up his mind.

"We'll let him loose. Let's see what kindness does for him."

Scott approached the dog, speaking softly.

"Better have a club handy," Matt warned.

Scott shook his head.

White Fang eyed Scott with suspicion. He had killed this man's dog. He had bitten his companion. He knew from experience that harsh punishment would follow. He bristled and bared his fangs.

The god held no club so he let him get closer than usual. The hand came forward. White Fang tensed. He knew the treachery of man-animals' hands.

Scott extended his hand. White Fang struck. Scott shouted with pain.

Matt ran to the cabin for a rifle.

"What are you doing?" Scott shouted.

"I said I would kill 'im if he didn't come around. And that's what I aim to do," Matt said. When he returned, Scott was there to stop him from hurting the wolf-dog. It was his turn to plead for White Fang's life.

"No!" Scott yelled. "You said we should give him a chance. We've only started. We

can't quit before we've even begun." He looked at his torn hand. "This time it served me right." Scott turned to White Fang. "And look at him!"

White Fang stood near the cabin snarling viciously. The blood-curdling growl was not directed at Scott. It was a clear warning to Matt and the rifle to watch out.

"Well, I'll be!" the dog-musher said.

"Look how intelligent he is." Scott said. "He knows guns as well as you do. If he's so intelligent, then he can surely learn new ways. We're going to give him a chance."

White Fang stopped snarling the moment the gun went down. Matt raised it again as a test. White Fang bared his teeth.

"I agree with you, Mr. Scott. That dog's too intelligent to kill."

The next day, Scott sat near White Fang. His injured hand was wrapped in a bandage, and his arm was in a sling. He carried no club or gun in his good hand. He spoke to White Fang in a comforting voice.

White Fang had never heard talk like that before. He was wary of the god who sat before him, but he listened to the quiet words. He began to feel secure. It was something he had never felt in the presence of men.

The god went into the cabin. He returned with a piece of meat. He held it out. White Fang was cautious. He knew from experience the hand could strike at any time. The god tossed the meat onto the snow. White Fang ate it. Nothing happened.

The god held out another piece of meat. White Fang approached it slowly. He kept his eyes on the god as he took the meat in his mouth. White Fang felt feelings from his dog nature that were thousands of years old.

The hand moved again. White Fang tensed, suspecting the worst. The urge to strike the hand was overwhelming, but another more powerful urge held him back. The hand was over his head. The sight of a fist was enough to pitch him into action. Instead, he laid his ears back and growled.

The hand petted him. Each time the

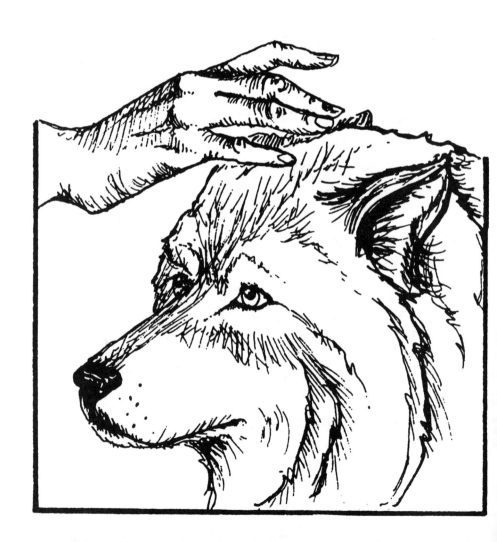

god raised his hand, White Fang expected a blow, but got a stroking that felt good.

Matt stepped out the cabin door. White Fang bristled and snarled. Scott resumed his stroking. The dog settled down. "Well, I'll be," Matt exclaimed.

White Fang's old life was over. A new, better, and much more fair life was opening. Weedon Scott had found his way into White Fang's soul with kindness. Like a key, the god's kindness unlocked something that was nearly dead in White Fang because it had never been nourished. It was his ability to love. It would not come in a single day. But it would come.

White Fang learned to be a new kind of dog. He learned the difference between thieves and honest men.

Weedon Scott went out of his way to be kind to the wolf-dog. He knew that much of White Fang's wrath was put there by other men who did not understand kindness.

White Fang accepted his petting. He even liked it. He could not stop growling,

but his growl was no longer a threat to Weedon Scott, though others might still think so.

White Fang was changing his ways. Instead of roaming the woods, he waited patiently at the empty cabin for his god to return.

He accepted Weedon Scott's caresses and his love, but he was too set in his

ways to show affection. He had never barked in his life, so he did not start now.

Trouble came in late spring. Weedon Scott packed a leather suitcase and disappeared. He did not return to the cabin, though White Fang waited patiently as always.

Matt took care of White Fang. He fed him just as Weedon Scott had, but it was not the same. White Fang would not eat. He became ill. He lay by the stove all day without moving. Matt began to worry. He wrote a letter to his employer who was on a trip to Circle City. "The wolf won't work," he wrote to Scott. "He won't eat. He doesn't fight with the other dogs. He doesn't know what happened to you and I don't know how to tell him. I think he might die."

A few nights later, Matt cocked his ear to the sound of approaching footsteps. The door opened and Weedon Scott stepped into the warm cabin. "Where's the wolf?" he asked.

Matt turned to the stove. "Holy smoke!" he exclaimed. "Would you look at him."

White Fang stood by the stove wagging his tail. Scott started across the room. White Fang met him in the middle.

Scott dropped to his knees and petted him fondly. White Fang's growl thrummed through the cabin. He thrust his head into his master's lap. He had never showed this kind of affection before in his life.

Scott's eyes glistened with love.

"I always said that wolf was a dog," Matt said excitedly. "Just look at 'im now."

White Fang recovered quickly. In two days he was as strong as ever. After that, life was pleasant. He returned his master's love by snuggling. His confidence in his god grew. He surrendered completely to Weedon Scott.

The two men were playing cards one night when a scream brought them to their feet. "The wolf's got somebody," Matt said.

Scott grabbed a lantern. He and Matt raced outside. A man lay in the snow, a prisoner of White Fang's blazing teeth.

Scott called off White Fang as Matt helped the man to his feet. It was Beauty Smith. In the snow was a steel dog-chain and a stout club.

Scott grabbed Beauty Smith's collar. He raised his fist. "You are not going to steal this dog," he said angrily. "Not now or ever!"

Beauty Smith turned on his heels and raced into the darkness.

Scott kneeled down to pet White Fang. "That's the last we'll ever see of him," he said.

CHAPTER

11

THE
SOUTHLAND

White Fang sensed something bad was happening. Weedon Scott and Matt went about their business as usual, but White Fang could feel it coming.

One night the two men were talking quietly after supper when Scott put his finger to his lips. "Listen," he whispered.

A low, sad moan drifted into the room, even though the door was closed. The men went outside. White Fang lay at the bottom of the stoop. He raised his eyes to his god. They were filled with despair.

"He knows something's up," Matt said.

Weedon Scott gazed first at the dog at his feet. Then he turned to Matt. "I can't take him with me," he said. "What can I do with a wolf in California?"

Matt shrugged his shoulders. He had no answer for his employer.

"The minute he saw a normal dog, he'd kill it on sight," Scott said. "I'd go bankrupt with lawsuits. The authorities would take him away and electrocute him. It would never do."

Matt nodded. "It would never do," he agreed. "But he does think a lot of you..."

"No!" Weedon Scott shouted. His rare anger betrayed the feelings he was fighting inside. He would have to give up White Fang. The thought troubled him. He calmed down. "I'm sorry, Matt. But I just can't take him."

"I know," Matt said. "But what gets me is how did he know you was goin'?"

"That just beats me," Scott said with a sad shake of his head.

The day came for Weedon Scott to leave for his home in California. His suitcase was packed and by the door. White Fang watched his master's every move. He grew more anxious as each minute passed. The last time his master had packed the suitcase and disappeared, he had been left behind. It was certain to be that way again. He dreaded each hour.

That night the men went to bed. Outside, White Fang trotted slowly to a small rise. He pointed his sleek muzzle toward the black sky, filled with twinkling

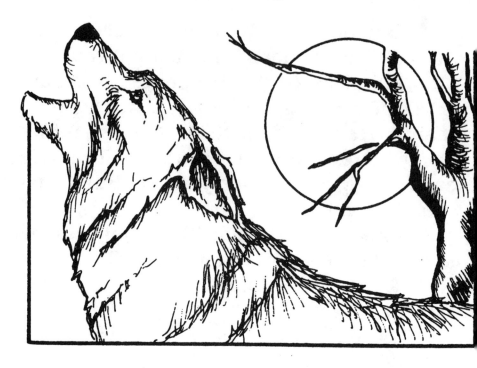

stars. He howled. He had done this only once before. It was when he was abandoned at the Indian camp after Gray Beaver and the others paddled away in their canoes. The howl was long and mournful. Its tragic song echoed across the vast Wild.

The men listened. "He's already off his food," Matt said. "The last time he nearly died. This time's goin' to be worse."

"Don't!" Weedon Scott shouted through the darkened room. "I can't take him with me. That's final!"

The next morning two Indians arrived at the cabin. The suitcase and canvas bags packed with Weedon Scott's belongings were ready. The Indians carried them off.

White Fang had trailed Weedon Scott all morning long. Now he waited by the door for his master to come out. But Scott called to White Fang to come inside. The dog entered.

Scott kneeled over him. He stroked his fur. He scratched his ears. He held White Fang's head, which was snuggled tightly against his lap.

The blast of a distant steamboat whistle shattered the silence.

"There she blows," Matt said. "There's not much time. Be sure to lock the front door. I'll go out the back. Let's go!"

Scott hurried out the front door and closed it quickly behind him as Matt did the same at the back door. White Fang was locked inside.

"Take good care of him," Weedon Scott said as the two men started down the hill toward the river.

"You can be sure I will," Matt replied.

Both men stopped short. A long, mournful howl rose from the cabin. It was the same sound a dog makes when its master dies. It was a heartbreaking sound that was interrupted only by short whines of misery and grief. The men hurried on without speaking.

The *Aurora* floated alongside the riverbank. It was the first steamboat of the year that would make the journey south. Gold-seekers and adventurers filled its decks. Some had made fortunes. Others were returning empty-handed.

Weedon Scott turned to Matt and extended his arm. The two men shook hands and said their good-byes. Scott was ready to step aboard the steamboat. His arm went limp as he studied the milling crowd on its deck. Sitting on his haunches in the center of the deck with a wistful look in his eye was White Fang.

"I'll take him ashore," Matt said. He moved toward White Fang. The wolf-dog shot between the legs of a group of startled men. Scott circled one way while Matt went the other. White Fang raced over the deck, eluding their grasps and ignoring their shouts.

Scott stopped. "Come," he ordered.

White Fang immediately went to his master's side. His nose had a fresh cut and another on his cheek dripped with blood.

"He went through the window to get here," Scott said.

"Must have butted straight through it," Matt added. The steamboat's whistle blew loudly above their heads. Matt reached for the dog. "I guess I'd better be gettin' him ashore with me," he said.

Scott stood up. He looked straight into his friend's eyes. "Good-bye, Matt, old man," he said. He turned his gaze to White Fang who sat obediently at his side. "But about the wolf. Well, you won't have to write me about him after all."

Matt's face burst into a wide-eyed smile. "You mean...?"

Scott nodded. "*I'll* have to write to *you* about him," he said. "White Fang is going home to California with me."

The whistle blew again. Matt raced down the gangplank which was hauled up the moment he stepped off. He waved a

final good-bye to his employer, but Weedon Scott was already kneeling at White Fang's side, scratching his ears with delight.

The steamer landed in San Francisco. White Fang stepped into a new land at the side of his master. The city was vastly different from the Northland. Tall buildings towered above their heads. The streets were filled with automobiles, carts, and people. Streetcars shrieked like angry lynxes.

They did not stay long. They went to the railroad station where Weedon Scott's bags were loaded into a baggage car. The god then put White Fang in the same car

with the bags. White Fang guarded his master's luggage and would not let anyone get close.

After a long and noisy ride, the train stopped. When the baggage-car door opened, White Fang saw a vastly different place. The city was gone. Sunshine warmed a broad, smiling countryside. Peace and quiet filled the air. The wolf-dog from the Wild did not understand how the change happened, but he was glad it had.

A carriage was waiting. Weedon Scott hurried to it, followed by White Fang. A man and a woman stepped off the carriage. The woman threw her arms around Scott.

White Fang's hair bristled. He snarled. To him the embrace was a hostile act. He leaped toward the woman. Scott stopped him an instant before the dog's fangs tore flesh. The woman jumped back in fear.

"It's all right, mother," Scott said as he calmed White Fang. "He was only protecting me. He'll learn."

The bags were loaded into the carriage. The people got in and with a crack of a whip, the horses broke into a trot. White Fang fell in behind the carriage. He glanced from side to side as he ran, watching to see that no harm came to his master in the carriage.

After a short ride, the carriage turned into a broad drive marked by a stone gate and flanked by long rows of arching walnut trees. On either side of the drive were sun-drenched hayfields glowing golden in midday light. In the distance rose tan hills dotted with dark green trees. A magnificent house stood at the end of the drive overlooking a broad valley.

There were too many things to see and

too little time for White Fang to see it. The moment the carriage entered the neatly trimmed grounds surrounding the house, a flash of white and brown raced out from hiding.

It was a sharp-muzzled sheepdog. Anger flashed in its eyes. It stopped between White Fang and Weedon Scott,

who was just stepping out of the carriage.

White Fang's hair bristled, but he did not move. The collie was a female. He could not attack. It was the law of his kind.

The collie did not recognize that law. She was driven by another that said wolves were a threat to the sheep her kind were raised to guard. She leaped at him.

White Fang backed away. The collie kept coming. White Fang turned. She pursued. No matter what he did, the collie was in White Fang's way.

The man in the carriage, Judge Scott,

called to the collie. "Here, Collie," he ordered.

Weedon Scott laughed. "Never mind, father. White Fang will have to learn for himself what is what. He may as well begin now."

The carriage continued to the house. White Fang and Collie were left behind, face to face. The collie did not let up, as

White Fang tried to circle around her. He turned again, but she was still there.

At last he gave in. He turned quickly and struck her sharply with his shoulder, his old fighting trick. The collie fell to the ground and rolled into a heap. She struggled to her feet, barking shrilly. She was not hurt, but her pride was damaged.

The way was clear. White Fang broke into a run toward the house where his master had gone. Nothing could catch him when it came to real running. The collie fell far behind.

White Fang raced around the corner of the house. A dark shape ran headlong into him. It was a large deer-hound. Their collision was unavoidable.

The hound plowed into White Fang's shoulder. The wolf fell to the ground. When he recovered his feet, his snout was curled into a fierce snarl. His ears lay flat back over the top of his head. His fangs glistened. He leaped for the hound.

Weedon Scott ran to separate the dogs before White Fang killed the hound. He

was too far away. The wolf poised for his fatal throat attack. An explosion of brown and white fur flew down the gravelled drive like a tornado. Collie hit White Fang in the side with her full weight. White Fang tumbled to the ground. The hound's life was spared.

Scott grabbed White Fang and calmed him. The wolf-dog quieted down under his master's gentle stroking. "This is a warm reception for a poor lone wolf from the Arctic," he said with a smile. "He's only been knocked off his feet once in his life, and here he's been rolled twice in thirty seconds."

White Fang tucked his muzzle into his

master's lap. Scott called to the hound. "Lie down, Dick!" he ordered.

Judge Scott approached. The collie and the hound eyed White Fang, and his were on them. "Let them fight it out," the judge said.

"If I do, you'll get a dead dog out of it," Scott warned. He led White Fang to the house. White Fang and the people entered. It was the other dogs that had to stay outside.

CHAPTER

12

THE GOD'S DOMAIN

Life at Sierra Vista, Judge Scott's estate, was good for White Fang. He quickly made himself at home. The dogs soon accepted him. Even Dick. White Fang had no love for any of them. All he wanted was for them to leave him alone. His snarls taught them to keep their distance.

Collie would not leave him in peace. She accepted his presence at Sierra Vista because that was her master's will. But the deeply buried memories of her own kind made White Fang an enemy. Through the ages, wolves had attacked the sheepfolds of her ancestors. She could not fight him because the gods of Sierra Vista would not permit it. But she could make his life miserable. Whenever she saw him, she picked on him. White Fang could do nothing but get out of her way.

Although White Fang was Weedon Scott's protector, he soon learned there were others at Sierra Vista he must also protect. Soon Weedon Scott's whole family became his responsibility. There was Judge Scott and his wife, Weedon's sisters, Beth and Mary, Weedon's wife Alice, and their two children, young Weedon and his sister Maude. White Fang guarded them equally because he knew they were loved by his master.

White Fang disliked children. Children in Indian villages had hurt him, so he distrusted all of the small people. Soon, however, he let young Weedon and Maude pet him. He didn't return their affection, but he didn't turn them away either. After a while, White Fang let the whole family pet him. But his own love was saved for his master.

There were other differences at Sierra Vista that White Fang had to learn. Sometimes his lessons came in the form of a scolding from his master's hand. But the blows were never delivered in anger, as the beatings had been in the Northland. They were only signs of his master's disapproval. Even then they were rare. Usually a sharp word was enough to drive a lesson home.

In the Northland, only dogs were tamed. Everything else roaming the forests was wild. That made them fair game for hunting. It was not so at Sierra Vista.

A stray chicken crossed White Fang's path one day. Because the chicken was running loose, White Fang attacked. A wild

bird was a meal, and he ate the fat chicken with gusto.

Later, when another pecked its way across the yard, he attacked again. This time a groom was nearby. The man held a whip. He was there to protect the chickens.

The whip cracked. White Fang crouched. His snout curled. His ears laid back. A deep, ugly growl came from his throat. His fangs glistened.

The whip cracked again. It stung sharply. White Fang leaped at the man's throat. The man fell backward, screaming with fear. The wolf-dog's fangs opened a cut in the man's arm all the way to the bone.

Collie raced around the corner and

headed straight for White Fang. The man cowered on the ground beneath the raging wolf, covering his throat with his good arm.

Collie snarled fiercely. White Fang backed off. The man scrambled to his feet and ran for safety. Collie did not let up. White Fang could not fight her. It was the law of his kind. He turned tail and fled across the fields.

"I'll have to teach him not to kill chickens," Weedon Scott said later, when the excitement died down. "But first I'll have to catch him in the act."

Two days later, White Fang sneaked into the chicken yard. Once he was inside, nothing on earth could save the chickens.

In minutes, fifty prize Leghorns were dead.

White Fang stood proudly over his kill as his master appeared. Scott's lips tightened. He spoke sharply. He grabbed the dog by the nape of his neck and forced his nose into the heap of dead chickens. He cuffed him soundly. White Fang never chased another chicken.

"You can't cure a chicken-killer once they've tasted blood." Judge Scott said sadly.

"You're wrong, father," Weedon Scott said. "I'll prove it. I'll lock White Fang in the chicken coop all afternoon and pay you a one-dollar gold coin for every chicken he kills."

"What if you win the bet?" Weedon's sister, Beth, asked. "Shouldn't father have to pay?"

"You're right," Weedon said. He thought for a moment. "This is your end of the bargain, father. If White Fang has not harmed a single chicken, you must speak to him just as you do to those you are sentencing in court. You must say, 'White Fang, you are smarter than I thought'."

The judge agreed. White Fang was locked in the coop. Weedon and the others left him completely alone. They did not

even stay nearby in hiding. White Fang eyed the milling chickens for a moment. Then he found a cool place in the dust and went to sleep.

Late that afternoon Judge Scott faced White Fang. The rest of the family was gathered on the porch behind him. "White Fang," the judge said solemnly. "You are smarter than I thought." He repeated his judgment sixteen times to the delight of everyone.

Wild animals were fair game for White Fang. He was allowed to hunt on his own or with his master who rode horseback ahead of him. In town, however, meat that hung in butcher shops was off limits. Cats, too, were not to be touched. And even the dogs had to be left alone.

When White Fang accompanied his master to town, people gathered to stare. He was very different from any dogs they knew. When they petted him, he had to permit it. The children were allowed to scratch his ears, too, but nobody dared to get too close to White Fang. He was, after

all, a wolf. He obeyed only because it was his master's wish.

Some of the townspeople tormented White Fang. One day this abuse went too far. The road to town passed a saloon, where men gathered idly in the shade. Three dogs were also there. Each time Weedon Scott rode by with White Fang close at his horse's heels, the men sicked the dogs on the wolf.

The wolf-dog's snarls kept them at a safe distance, but they badgered him mercilessly. This went on for many days. At last Weedon acted. He stopped his horse

and turned to White Fang. "Go to it," he said.

White Fang leaped at the dogs. His fighting tactics were as sharp as when he used them in the Yukon. The three dogs stood shoulder to shoulder, their teeth bared, poised and ready. White Fang struck.

A dust storm erupted around the raging animals. The men at the saloon and Weedon Scott on the road watched, but could see nothing. Growling, snarling, and the clash of teeth came from inside the dust cloud. When it settled, two dogs lay dead. The third was badly hurt. It tried to run away, but White Fang knocked it to the ground and finished it off.

Weedon Scott continued into town. White Fang followed. The men returned to the saloon. It did not take many days for word of the slaughter to spread up and down the valley. White Fang never was troubled by dogs again.

White Fang lived a comfortable life at Sierra Vista. Human kindness had changed him. He accepted his new life eagerly. Inside still ran the blood of a wolf, but he was now more dog than wild animal. He was content with the change.

He remained aloof and alone, however. The memory of persecution by Lip-lip and the pack of puppies in his youth was still strong. So was his hatred of the fighting dogs he battled under Beauty Smith's evil guidance.

Collie refused to become friendly with him and would not leave him alone. She trailed him like a police officer, barking a sharp warning if he dared to idly glance at a chicken. White Fang's only escape was to lie down, cover his head with his forepaws, and pretend to be asleep.

Weedon Scott rode his horse often. One of White Fang's duties and great pleasures was to follow the horse over the rolling hills. He could run fifty miles without tiring. He did so in silence, because White Fang never barked. Then the day came when he had to.

The master was riding at a gallop

across a broad meadow many miles from Sierra Vista. White Fang ran behind, keeping pace with the horse's flashing hooves.

Without warning, a jackrabbit bounded across the horse's path. Startled, the horse turned suddenly. It fell heavily to the ground, throwing Weedon Scott into a heap. The sharp crack of a breaking bone and Scott's cry of pain told the story.

Scott struggled to get up. It was useless. "Go home," he shouted at White Fang.

White Fang circled his master. It was

his job to protect, not to abandon. "Go home, wolf," Scott commanded. "Tell them to come!"

White Fang knew the meaning of "home." He turned tail and raced over the hills toward the estate.

It was late afternoon when he arrived. "Weedon's home," Weedon's mother said when she saw White Fang. The children tried to pet him. He pushed them away.

The family studied the wolf-dog's strange behavior, but soon ignored him.

White Fang grabbed Alice Weedon's skirt and tugged. She reacted with fear. She was very much aware of White Fang's history. White Fang let go. His body trembled. He opened his jaws, but no sound came out.

"I do believe he's trying to speak," Alice Weedon said.

White Fang's frozen throat melted. He barked loudly until everyone realized the truth.

"Something has happened to Weedon!" Alice cried.

Thanks to White Fang, his master's life was saved.

After the rescue, White Fang's own life was better than ever. He held a special place in everyone's heart. Even Collie became friendly. Soon they were playing together. By the end of his second winter at Sierra Vista, White Fang and Collie were inseparable.

One day they ran off to the woods together, just like White Fang's father, old One-Eye, and his mother, Kiche, had done years before in the Wild. When they returned, they were forever side-by-side.

Soon after, the story of a daring prison escape filled the local paper. A convict had broken out of San Quentin Prison. His name was Jim Hall. He was a brutal man. He killed two guards while making his escape, and he took their weapons with him. A reward in gold was placed on his head. The people of the region took down their own guns to hunt him.

Jim Hall disappeared. No sight or trace of him was found. People were deathly afraid. But at Sierra Vista, the man who had most reason to be afraid merely laughed. Judge Scott was the judge who sentenced Jim Hall to jail for his crimes in the first place. Hall had sworn revenge.

Alice Scott was as frightened of the news of Jim Hall's escape as the rest of the people in the region. To quiet her fears, she secretly got out of bed each night after the household was asleep and let White Fang inside. The wolf was allowed to sleep in the great hall until morning when she let him out. Nobody was the wiser.

One night White Fang's sleep was disturbed by an unwelcome scent. He tested the air. A strange god had entered the house. It was someone who did not belong. His ears perked as the sounds of the stranger's footsteps drifted through the silent hall. He rose to his feet. Keeping well hidden in the darkness, he waited.

The stranger entered the hall. White Fang's keen eyes followed him across the room. The man stopped at the stairway to the second floor where White Fang's family lay asleep.

The hair on White Fang's neck bristled. His snout curled, but he did not snarl. His ears lay flat over the top of his head. His eyes focussed sharply on the figure at the foot of the stairs. When the man started up the stairway, White Fang leaped forward. In an instant he was at the man's throat.

The family awoke to the sound of an uproar. Fierce growling and snarling and the terrified shouts of a man shattered the quiet. There was a gunshot, and then two more. As fast as it started, the commotion ceased. Weedon Scott raced down the stairs. He turned on the lights.

A man lay at the bottom of the steps. His throat was torn open. He was dead. White Fang lay in a heap a few feet away.

Scott turned the man over to expose his face. "Jim Hall!" he gasped. Then he went to White Fang.

The dog was gasping for breath. His eyes were half-shut. Scott patted his neck, but White Fang could not move. Suddenly the dog went limp. Scott shook his head sadly. "He's done for," he sighed.

Judge Scott stepped forward. He picked up the telephone. "We'll see about that," he said.

A short time later, the surgeon summoned by the judge's call was working feverishly over the dying wolf-dog. "He has one chance in a thousand to survive," he said. He counted the injuries. "A broken hind leg, three broken ribs, a pierced lung, and three bullet holes clear through him." He shook his head sadly.

"Never mind the expense to save him," the judge exclaimed.

"He shall get the best treatment," the doctor said. "But even that may not be enough. He needs to be nursed just as you would care for a sick child. Do that. I'll be back later this evening."

The doctor left. Weedon Scott and the others immediately turned their attention to the badly injured dog. They would nurse him back to health themselves.

White Fang lay bandaged for many weeks. He slept and dreamed. In his dreams he roamed the Wild with Kiche. He hunted again with Gray Beaver. He ran for his life from Lip-lip and the dog pack. He fought dogs and suffered the blows of

Beauty Smith. He snarled and whimpered as a flood of memories of his early life disturbed his sleep.

One day the dreams stopped. White Fang awoke to the tender touch of human hands. They were removing the bandages and cutting off the casts.

Weedon Scott rubbed White Fang's ears. "Blessed Wolf," Alice Scott said. The whole family and all the others of Sierra Vista, as well, gathered for this happy day.

White Fang struggled to his feet. He

stood on wobbly legs, embarrassed to be so weak.

"No ordinary dog could have done what he did," Judge Scott crowed proudly. "White Fang is a wolf!"

White Fang walked gingerly to the door. The family followed him outside. He headed toward the stable. Collie was in the yard. Six fat puppies romped in the warm sunshine at her feet. Their coats were gray, like their father's. Collie stood over the puppies like a defiant guard. She snarled a warning at White Fang.

One of the puppies scooted from under Collie's protective eye. It ran to White Fang's feet and flopped on its back. Collie stiffened, ready to leap to the pup's rescue.

White Fang pressed his nose against the puppy's soft belly. The puppy licked his face with its tiny red tongue. White Fang blinked. He licked the puppy's face with his own. The other puppies ran forward. Collie let them go. White Fang lay down on the ground and let them climb all over him as he drowsed peacefully in the warm glow of the afternoon sun.

The wolf-dog of the Wild had found peace and happiness at last.

THE END

ABOUT THE AUTHOR

JACK LONDON was born on January 12, 1876 in San Francisco, California. As a child, he lived on ranches and spent time on the waters of San Francisco. Then, in his teens, he went to sea and became an oyster pirate.

After working odd jobs and getting into trouble with the law, Jack London began to value education. Studying very hard, he tried to cram both a high school and college education in just a few months.

Then, gold was discovered in 1897 in the Klondike, a river valley located in the Yukon Territory of Canada. Twenty-one-year-old London hiked the six-hundred miles there from California to find his fortune. But after spending a very cold winter in the Far North, without finding any gold, he decided to return to San Francisco and take up writing.

The best known writer of his time, Jack London produced many adventure stories and novels, including *The Call of the Wild*, *The Sea Wolf*, and *White Fang*.

The Young Collector's
Illustrated Classics

Adventures of Robin Hood
Black Beauty
Call of the Wild
Dracula
Frankenstein
Heidi
Little Women
Moby Dick
Oliver Twist
Peter Pan
The Prince and the Pauper
The Secret Garden
Swiss Family Robinson
Treasure Island
20,000 Leagues Under the Sea
White Fang